_hydrus

Copyright © 2021 Hydrus
Cover Copyright © 2021 Hydrus

All rights reserved.

The characters depicted in this book are fictitious. Any similarity to real persons, living or dead, is coincidental and not intended by the author.

The scanning, uploading, and distribution of this book without permission is a theft of the author's intellectual property. If you would like permission to use material from the book (other than for review purposes), please contact hydruspoetry@gmail.com. Thank you for your support of the author's rights.

Published by: Hydrus
Photography & Illustrated Art by: Hydrus
Cover Design by: Cleo Moran - Devoted Pages Designs
Formatting by: Cleo Moran - Devoted Pages Designs
https://www.devotedpages.com
Proofreading: Amina Jojo Dahmouche

Manufactured in the United States of America

The Library of Congress Cataloging-in-Publication Data is available upon request.

Paperback ISBN: 978-1-7357824-9-2
E-Book ISBN: 978-1-7357824-8-5

_hydrus

Dedicated to those who love
To those who hurt in love
And to those who would hurt all over again
Just for the experience of being in love

ENDlove ENDpain

Is my latest collection of poems that deal with the human struggle of being in love. The emotional roller coaster and the ups and downs that our souls take on this journey. This path is one of endless bliss but sometimes agony.

Love is always a conflict of raw emotion and trust. It is a journey we seek to take and at times we regret we do. It is a struggle between good vs. evil but mostly in ourselves.

An overthinking paradox of what to do, how to be, what was done, and what will never possibly be. Regardless of the experiences, they will always shape who we are. Those feelings will stay with us forever. They are etched as reminders in our very being.

Never to be erased but only to be hidden. They are made up of thoughts and memories that pierce our dreams, fill our fantasies and fill the voids in our hearts. They affect us mentally and sometimes physically.

Lifes etchings, bruises, and scars we all hold as witnesses to this spell we call Love.

When those who love you scatter

_hydrus

Call on me
I am here
Always alert
To fight your fears

On this day
Like all the rest
Trust your hero
With every test

I will avenge
Slice their heads
Kill the snakes
Retake their beds

Paint their venom
On our tongues
Dip the quivers
Write our songs

In the battle
We will prevail
Sword still drawn
All breaths exhaled

We will triumph
Upon their corpse
Insert the flag
Show no remorse

Stages
_hydrus

Little box
What do you hold
What is locked
What cannot be told

Your secrets grim
Or full of lies
The keys are lost
Yet no one cries

Who holds the answers
To whats inside
Are there clues
To why we die

Can it just open
So we can see
Life has some meaning
My effigy

Empty
_hydrus

Let me strangle your demons
Crush them under my wings
Scorch them all to ashes
Watch them burn within

Them
_hydrus

My bones
Dress the lawn
To feed the worms
From all thats gone

It marks the path
Where I am laid
Buried under
Just to decay

In this ground
I live to be
An immortal part
Of a loving tree

In its roots
Connect my veins
Through the air
I reach the rains

And feed myself
From the clouds
Thunder sparks
They crash so loud

I grow again
Then fruit I bear
Where you then eat
Live my despair

Ingest
_hydrus

Where have you gone
Only in mirrors you hide
A reflection of truth
Erased by your side

Empty my hand
Only a shadow it holds
Reaching for nothing
We only grow cold

Shatter
_hydrus

On this day
I made my bed
Awoke the shadows
From which I fed

They laid me down
For my retreat
I say farewell
Until we meet

Slumber
_hydrus

My black heart
Beats alone
It reeks of havoc
Withered to stone

Weathered vessel
Contains my curse
In its chamber
Remains one verse

A slow repeat
Its cryptic thump
Melodic sleep
Of a horrid slump

The webs ordain
Covered with dust
Bloody the stains
Iron with rust

Broken the chest
No more convulse
Full of regret
Faint the pulse

Dimly it cries
In a moaning wain
Never to find love
It mourns in pain

Organ
_hydrus

I took a walk
Through the woods
The trees were bare
Where all stood

Looking away
One heard a scream
A widowed woman
Grave the dream

Once I awoke
By the roots
The bark had rotted
Stained my boots

Unaware
Of what was spilled
My bloodied hand
Exposed my guilt

Wanderer
_hydrus

Lift me angel
From the spear
Impaled again
Death grows near

Your wings can take me
So far away
Judged once more
The price was paid

Dim the sight
Hear the horns
Golden chalice
Awaits the scorned

As I reach
To unlock the gate
I plunge to hell
All my sins await

As I tumble
Back upon my blade
I stare at heaven
And all of my mistakes

They watch and smile
Amused by their loss
How dare I seek
Now I bear the cross

Judas
_hydrus

You took my petals just to watch me bleed
Now you ride my thorns to inject your seed

_hydrus

From these leaves
I picked a flower
Its thorns were sharp
It had such power

Its cuts were few
But oh so deep
A constant slice
Grown to repeat

I added water
For it to bloom
This sprouted feelings
A relentless gloom

The sun then jaded
Dried the skies
The petals faded
Inside I died

Replanted
_hydrus

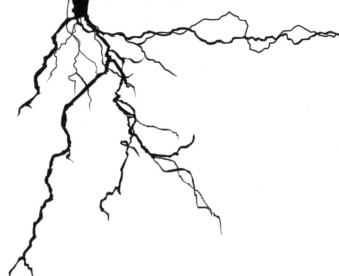

Where will I be
On this cloudy day
Enjoying some tea
As I simply decay

Or will I just stare
Into the empty dark sky
Wishing for thunder
To strike my own life

Horizon
_hydrus

May the crows
Eat my eyes
Dine on me
As I die
Let me hang
With no remorse
My final act
Took its course
I dont beg
I dont cry
Just am still
Under the sky
I just wait
I just pray
This final act
This final day

Here
_hydrus

Let the demons
Take my soul
Feast on my voices
A binging untold
So not worthy
Of pity
Or grief
I am the unholy
A heart full of thieves

Swiped
_hydrus

Dress me in soil
It makes my own bed
Caressing the dreadful
That lives in my head

Shovel my passion
Trenched to deceive
Vacant the lifeless
Conceived to mislead

Treachery
_hydrus

Let my rose wilt
 for it lives in the shadows of others

_hydrus

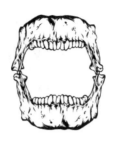

Abandoned skin
Draped on a chair
Lifelessly bruised
Irrationally bare

Marked by your winter
Frozen in touch
Flaked by confusion
Unwilling the crush

A coldness inside
Birthed from the bone
Posed in defiance
Butchered on stone

Left for the flies
Eagerly they wait
Blood for the course
I was their play

Meat
_hydrus

Knuckles clenched
As I wait
Tonight will be
His final date

In his sight
I will be
Carving out
My legacy

Painted blood
Hollowed pleas
The mind succumbs
To my greed

I still feel pain
No remorse
My fists proclaim
To take their course

Vengeance
_hydrus

In your ocean
I battled waves
Drowned by murder
For countless days

Yet I swam back
To fight the tide
Unknown to me
You always lied

Rivals
_hydrus

Little doll
Dressed in blue
Thrown away
For something new

May the hands
That tore your dress
Meet a fate
That never rests

Have them burn
Set ablaze
Let them scream
Ignite on stage

We will watch
To see them die
Burn in hell
With all your lies

Done
_hydrus

Even in silence
The mob will chant
Search for crumbs
Pounce like ants
Create a voice
Without speech
A tyrants rule
To always preach
I close my eyes
Cover the sounds
Pounding away
Destroying ground
Until they tread
Upon my chest
They want me dead
Just laid to rest

Swarmed
_hydrus

    Quietly
The shadows blend
    Silently
There lives my end
    Reluctantly
I dropped my knife
    Defiantly
She took my life

    Knowingly
    _hydrus

Meet my friend
Its misery
It found a place
Inside my tree

I built its nest
There they live
Hugging me tight
Ready to give

Never selfish
It knows no end
Listens to me
This constant friend

There they are
Waiting to muse
For if I win
I will also lose

Constant
_hydrus

Why pretend
All is great
The universe laughs
Watching our fate

We try to run
Through this celestial maze
An enchanted test
Under an infinite gaze

All fall and bleed
These are the rules
Just mend the wounds
Gather your tools

For in this quest
You never find your way
Once you just appear
Your day fades away

Vanished
_hydrus

Dripping venom
Toothless grin
Biding smile
Digested in

Feeding fluid
Meant for life
Scalpel spineless
Twisted knife

On my bed
A studied foe
Sliced for fun
A new john doe

Victim
_hydrus

In the sky
Fly my sons
Circling demons
One by one
When I call
They quickly strike
Tasting blood
With every bite
Every peck
Their horde expels
So many chants
And wicked spells
On this night
Cried the sun
Bloodied feathers
Their flight was done

Avenge
_hydrus

I met her
In a darkened room
Full of pain
And tortured doom
Every wall
Spoke of lies
Mirrors laughed
Curtains cried
Will I ever
Get a key
Unlock the hell
Of agony
Or simply wait
For my bed
Prepare the knife
To slice the head

Wait
_hydrus

In my cave
With the dead
I dwell all day
In my head

Voices speak
And play their games
Planting thoughts
As mischief reigns

No inner peace
Just vast denial
Unchained the beast
Awaiting trial

The inner demons
I cant avoid
Allured by sadness
They fill my void

Partners
_hydrus

She left me to rot
Broke all my bones
Dug up the grave
Then filled it with stones
I never was found
As the worms ate away
My soul keeps whole
As I slowly decay

Punished
_hydrus

Awake I stare
As sleep escapes
An abandoned glare
Night cannot wait
Arms slowly turn
A deathly pace
My conscience mourns
All ones mistakes

Burdened
_hydrus

Fog covers
All I see
An endless curtain
Of misery

It covers my soul
Captures my breath
Taking its toll
Baiting my death

In it I fly
Talons in wait
Vigil to gut
All those I hate

Yet silence in flight
I maneuver my wings
Dance with the reaper
As we both start to sing

Grim
_hydrus

Deadly flowers
Watch the skies
Your little friends
Are raining lies

As the storms
Rise to breach
Alone again
Life lessons teach

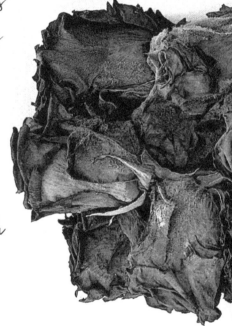

Envious
_hydrus

Pick the stone
You wish to throw
Aim at me
With all you know

Watch the rock
Bruise the beast
Its my turn
To remove the leash

Bite
_hydrus

In my bones
Memories evade
Scattered thoughts
Ideas fade
Small glimpses
Of scattered lies
Overthinking
Inside I cry
All is futile
It comes in waves
Nightmare haunts
Tortured days
As I lay
In my pool
The ceiling crumbled
Killed the fool

Circumstance
_hydrus

Let me be
Your skeleton
I have
Several of my own
Not living
Is my specialty
Dying
Is what I own
Life is just a journey
Trivial in fact
A joke to those
Who know me
Regardless
Of the facts

Reckless
_hydrus

Step into
My shallow grave
It fits two
I cant behave

Misfortune
_hydrus

My corpse lays still
As the world applauds
Inking for thrills
Unjust the cause
All will bleed
Pretend the pain
Unknown to me
Its all the same

Used
_hydrus

Black sun rises
Only to fall
Eclipsed by the moon
Those who know all
Left by the shadows
Dragged through the rain
Caged is my raven
Drowning in pain

Sunsets
_hydrus

Where did you go
Life took you from me
Left was a shell
A lost harmony

Mute was the spirit
Vacant the glare
Emotions evicted
Alone unaware

Desperately seeking
A voice or a sound
Nothing was breathing
Pounding the ground

Loss was embedded
Shape me into stone
I also live vacant
Awake and alone

Gone Again
_hydrus

I miss you again
The stories you told
The time that we spent
We were to grow old

Life played us so cruel
Ended our game
Took you from me
And all that remained

Stories are few
Time is just time
Memories of you
And all that was mine

Here left to my thoughts
And losing my friend
I am missing you still
Again and again

Always
_hydrus

I have opened
What I cant bear
I lost my soul
All that was dear

Its just so hard
To lay and wait
The day never came
Where you stayed awake

Slipped
_hydrus

Today I drowned
On my own
Inside my thoughts
Within my bones
With such ease
It takes my breath
Replayed events
Pretending death
Thats how it feels
When the lonesome cries
No one hears
Because no one dies
They just live on
In a trampled corpse
Their crime was love
Without remorse

Battered
_hydrus

Do you think of me
As I am thinking of you
Just wasting away
Nothing left to do
I rot in wait
And overthink
Doubts contemplate
My heart simply sinks

Done
_hydrus

Darkness is the light I know
It shines on me when I am low
Bleeds my heart into the night
Carries me when I cant fight
Gives me love when I fail
Drapes my skin in a wounded veil
Holds me up when I wont stand
Takes the knife out of my hand

Protected
_hydrus

I cant breathe
Without your breath
Holding me
As we wept
Longing for
Another day
Time was cruel
You slipped away

Sleep
_hydrus

Today I held
A photograph
It took me back
To a distant past

I ran away
When I caught a glimpse
Of what was pure
Has not been since

Running
_hydrus

Judge me for the tears you caused
but will never see me reveal

_hydrus

Drink from my veins
They bleed without hope
A lonely existence
One that cant cope
Buried in anguish
It melts just to drain
Unwilling to triumph
My ink only stains

Unwritten
_hydrus

Living in a bloody pool
Dancing demons found their fool
In my thoughts they cry in pain
Leaving one to go insane

Sleepless
_hydrus

Will the birds sing today
Sunlight seems so far away
Caged in pain they eat the seeds
Never wanting to be freed

Habit
_hydrus

My empty seat begs for your return

_hydrus

Random notes
Sketched in ease
Posted pages
Made just to tease

Feelings jotted
Ignoring pain
A failed attempt
Nothing to gain

Ignore
_hydrus

Only the tears
Can claim my space
Falling to earth
Leaving their trace

Reddening eyes
As hands reach my face
Lonely in life
Forgotten my place

Isolated
_hydrus

When will I find
That safe space
The one that heals
Covers my trace
Hides me from those
Who hurt me so
Quietly I
Must let go

Cannot
_hydrus

Tell me something
I do not know
About the time
So long ago
We lived before
Once upon
I reminiscence
But all is gone

Remember
_hydrus

Waves in the distance
A crashing arrest
Torrential your path
You vanquish my best

I swim with your current
Blind to your will
You dismember my voyage
And rejoice at the thrill

I drown in your envy
Float to your rocks
Jagged the entry
Unconsciously docked

Yet mute is your silence
I awake to your rains
My path will continue
As you laugh at my pain

Dive
_hydrus

The depths hide my demons
They wander in my space
Devouring my feelings
Consuming me to taste

Their leash is ever growing
Its grip strengthens to choke
It begs for me to tighten
I struggle just to cope

On my back they trample
Stomping me to waste
My anguish is their temple
Whipping me in haste

On my knees I struggle
Clawing as I bleed
Helpless in this torture
Voraciously they feed

Enslaved
_hydrus

I kept your flowers
Close to my bed
They watched me sleep
Their pain I fed

I cant believe
That you are gone
Night stays with me
And keeps me numb

Render
_hydrus

I fell
I fall
I tumbled
I crawled

Regrets
So many
The guilt
Just killed me

Roman
_hydrus

Laying down
On a grassy field
Closed my eyes
Cannot deal
Pleading for
A baited moon
Became the stalk
To meet my doom

Harvest
_hydrus

Piercing needles
Strike my back
Bracing for
A new attack

Heaven plagued
To cleanse my sin
Inside the host
One kills within

Baptized
_hydrus

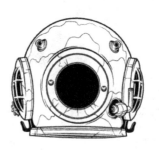

Thunder claps
In the night
Etching ink
As I write
Fallen heads
Crack the skull
My emotions
Never call
Beating with
Angry words
Too numb
And too absurd
I crawl back
Into my state
In the abyss
I sadly wait

Depths
_hydrus

I am
The blade
A critic
To blame

Sarcastic
Inside
I crumble
My name

The truth
A tremble
My beat
Grew silent

All air
Felt distant
Smothered
Defiant

Stubborn
_hydrus

Take the laugh
From this clown
Life has turned
Him upside down
Foolish cards
Tried to predict
His awkward smile
Was his best trick

Finale
_hydrus

Why do thoughts
Question me
Whisper secrets
That cannot be
Why must I
Always fail
To have the strength
And just prevail

Failed
_hydrus

Dragons wings
Castles burn
Morbid shields
Tides have turned
Casted spells
Bloodshot eyes
Hurling spears
The dead arrives
Take my soul
Battered deeds
Hang the martyrs
Watch them bleed
Holy ghosts
Broken crowns
Another Reign
Has come down

Camelot
_hydrus

She surprised me with forever
Then my demons broke her heart

Asshole
_hydrus

Why do you continue to haunt
An abandoned house
Where not even the memory of your ghost
Resides

Residual
_hydrus

One never feels abandoned
Until they are reminded that they were

_hydrus

I lived in her coffin
An amused corpse with a pulse

_hydrus

There is no more
Left to give
When all we give
Comes from a broken heart

Wounded
_hydrus

I searched
For what
Was missing
Knowing
All along
It was gone
We never
Held each other
Even though
Our hearts
Were one

Vacant
_hydrus

Oh sad cruelty
Disguised as an angel
Giving me shelter
From darkness
With its wings
Pretending to be
Righteous
Judging all my shadows
Even though their inner evil
Is all she sings

Charlatan
_hydrus

There is a hungry soul
That keeps me warm
With her rivers
That paint my storm

She lets me drown
Then fades away
Its a game
She vilely plays

Selfish
_hydrus

In the distance
Is where I breathe
Left alone
In the place I bleed
Too many hauntings
Too many ghosts
I am meant to be banished
Far from any and most

Exiled
_hydrus

I dont deserve
Another chance
Having burned the roads
Thrown away the maps

I am always lost
Myself to blame
Nothing matters
Life with no name

Anonymous
_hydrus

You made us into a complicated question
Now leaving you is the simple answer

_hydrus

Slashes
Tears
Burns
And cuts
Dressing skin
In lifes mistrust

Sadly one
Feels no pain
Living for
The dripping rain

Red
_hydrus

Every word
That is felt
It lives inside
Before its dealt

A silent brew
Of questioned reels
Stirs in wait
Taunts ordeal

Then in a hush
A mute reply
It culminates
Unknown the why

Yet there it sits
Unleashed to all
Why did I speak
Just to fall

Replayed
_hydrus

I will carry your cross
  along with the one I currently bear
                              _hydrus

Carry me away
Legs cannot move
Their will is broken
Movement is few

I need not mend
Or fix my stride
I lost my friend
Inside I died

Blinked
_hydrus

Little voice inside my head
Waits for me beside my bed
Telling me lets start the day
Questioning why I awake

Everyday
_hydrus

I am bitter
I am rage
I am sad
Inside my cage

No more keys
To my bars
A trapped reminder
Of your scars

Held
_hydrus

Why cant I feel okay
When the sun comes out to play
I only watch the clouds
They scream and are so loud

Dark
_hydrus

Drain the wells
Tongues have ceased
Words now emptied
No more released
They swam away
Down a rivers path
Nothing to say
Drowned in their wrath

Speechless
_hydrus

My serpent friend
Your poison drips
I smell its stench
Where I once sipped

You curl in wait
Watching what moves
Ignoring rats
Collecting clues

You search at night
Under the beds
Dangling hands
Confess the dead

You slip away
I feel your tongue
The bite was quick
All is undone

Oiled
_hydrus

Screams they chant
And call the slave
Another time
To misbehave
All they do
Is bite the hand
Never safe
To discipline

Strike
_hydrus

Wounded games
And fractured hearts
Mental pains
So far apart
Innocence
Perceived to skew
Jealousies
Undid the two

Petty
_hydrus

I built a cage that only your

Ramblings voiced
Behind a muse
Suspicious whispers
Made to confuse
Ill intent
To deceive the choir
Karma claims
Another liar

Predictable
_hydrus

Far from me
She escapes to write
Showing the world
Her uncensored fight

Bleeding games
All of lifes misdeeds
Baiting masses
With her feed

They will eat
All will beg
Thirsting more
Gorging dread

Sadly the soul
Continues to die
Finding friends
Amongst the lies

Social
_hydrus

On the ground
I stare and wait
A distant stare
I contemplate

Dreaming of us
All that can be
Our daily lives
Eternity

In this daze
One overthinks
Doubts the heart
Then starts to sink

How can it be
I missed the clues
You chose me
To believe the ruse

Reality
_hydrus

All her words
Conceal the tools
That lead me to
Be her fool

They cracked my spine
Tore my core
Inhaled my ribs
And left me sore

Brittle bones
Ripped off flesh
I was all eaten
The meat was fresh

In a pile
Wained my desire
She lit the match
Then put out the fire

Dined
_hydrus

Take your pics
Expose your life
Play the muse
The worlds good wife

All will see
Behind the glass
Posting scenes
That never last

Mental pictures
Portray the acts
Words adorn
Conveying facts

The ridicule
Will seem unfair
Asking for likes
The bullshits clear

Together
_hydrus

Bleed empty tears
Paint the walls
Blame disease
For the fall
The sharpened knives
Were dull with faith
Mistrust in all
Secured our fate

Tidal
_hydrus

Spill your heart
As I bleed
Enjoy the freedom
Of a dying seed
Let the masses
Watch in haste
Feed my sadness
As I burn in waste

Dredge
_hydrus

Tell me how
This should end
You seem to know
Every bend
I trip and fall
To find my place
You just move on
At your own pace
Quickly I walk
Then start to run
Its not enough
To chase the sun
One cannot win
There was no start
Began too late
Worlds far apart
So let me sit
Enjoy the view
My race has ended
Its overdue

Relay
_hydrus

You will never know
What you meant to me
I was misunderstood
A tree without leaves

Casting no shadow
No cover from rain
Simply just standing
Eclipsing your pain

Trying to grow
To reach every spot
Regardless the storms
I caught every last drop

Yet there I stood
No matter the weeds
Rotting my wood
You taking with greed

Soon getting an ax
Mistrust covered the blade
Slicing my soul
No longer in shade

Uprooted
_hydrus

Angels blessed me with her love
My demons carried her away

_hydrus

The stars aligned
And played her song
Crying tears
Of what went wrong
Lonely feels
Tragic its fate
All is fine
No one will wait

Left
_hydrus

Coat me with your sins... So my skin can confess
_hydrus

Why do I bleed
These empty words
I felt the need
So ill absurd
I was the cause
To every scar
Now life just hit
You are so far

Away
_hydrus

Open arms
Unedited speech
I fell for her
She felt my reach

Great the bond
Distant the touch
Doubts arose
It was too much

What quickly grew
Then caught aflame
All was too new
I was to blame

Now in my hole
Im left to sleep
Away from all
Its where
I weep

Imposed
_hydrus

She left
She is gone
I pushed her away
I was wrong
In the end
My heart still grieves
It knows the truth
Why did she leave

Mistake
_hydrus

No more laughter
Funny things
Morning kisses
As we sing
Just empty sheets
Full of forgotten stains
Where once you laid
And we made it rain

Abandon
_hydrus

I think of you
Do you think of me
We were so right
It could not be
How did the world
Just crush our dreams
I was never meant
Never meant to be

False
_hydrus

Dripping candle
Hot in wax
Burning knuckles
As I act

Pouring pleasure
From the heat
Slowly dowsing
No retreat

Spreading fire
A lighted gloom
Smoke gets thicker
Impending doom

What was pleasure
Turns to fear
Ill keep pouring
As you tear

Trial
_hydrus

Unwanted distraction
Played just to fill
Every hole
That wasnt drilled

False intentions
Prepped to fail
Another game
For a phallus tale

Unknown
_hydrus

Under your sheets
My fingers beg
Slow is their search
Upon your legs

They famishedly trace
A scent is reached
Hands are placed
They found their peace

Lured
_hydrus

Fingers write
They tend to brush
Retrace the steps
Of those they touch

Define our light
Needle to weave
Embrace the night
Then they leave

In us they breathe
Born from trust
Spilled with tears
Read with trust

Marked
_hydrus

Let me be your wings
 A rock to stand on
When the world sinks

        Hold On
        _hydrus

On this table
We always ate
With our mouths
Without plates

Here the wood
Marks your spot
Hungry hands
Tied their knots

Drenched in oil
Cut the knives
Dipped the spoon
Looked in your eyes

We served each other
On this bed
Inside forever
We always fed

Full
_hydrus

Arch your back
Open wide
Let me see
Where I will slide
Breathless moan
Clenching gape
I must consume
Eat every shape
Push me in
Mark my face
As I lick
Every trace
Lets devour
As we pinch
Take me whole
Every inch

Breakfast
_hydrus

I live for the arch in your back

Where your sweat settles on my hands

_hydrus

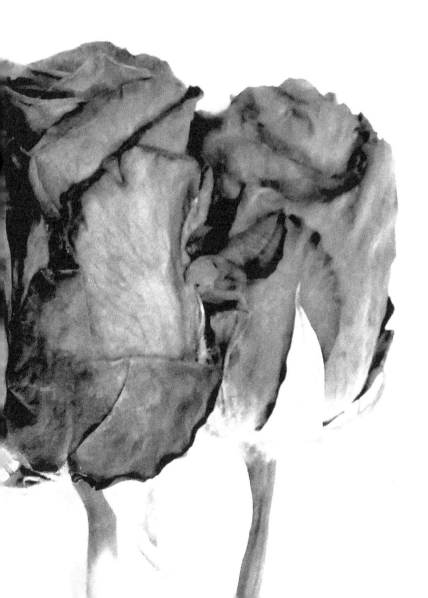

Here I lay
Inside my den
Stroking the fire
That lives within

It breathes for you
And calmly waits
For you to come
Onto my plate

Enter
_hydrus

Take your ropes
Tie my wrists
Blindfold my eyes
Enjoy the twist

Belt the flesh
Drain my veins
Lust and lick
Inflict your pain

Enjoy your muse
Your ridden corpse
Extract your ink
Reply your worse

Shattered bat
On a table lay
Reflect in glory
I will have my day

Vow
_hydrus

In your cauldron
I only dive
Swim in juices
Keep us alive

Possessed in spirit
As I drink
Turn your stew
In you I sink

Spell
_hydrus

Taste my lips
They taste of you
Taste our flesh
And all we do

I live for this
And want you to
Taste again
I taste of you

Loops
_hydrus

Only her hands
Belonged on me
It knew my strengths
And every need

It rubbed my skin
And felt my chest
Gripped my arms
Muscles and pecs

Rode my bones
Wrapped her legs
Squeezed the moans
That made us beg

Took me in
To coat my spill
Inside every core
We ravaged our will

Owned
_hydrus

Let me pinch your spot
Rub it with my thumb
Leave yourself wide open
Watch you slowly come

Let me take myself
Playing with your lips
Gripping what is yours
Pressing on my tip

Coating all your fingers
Driving them so deep
Let me hear your bliss
Dripping as I seep

Immersed
_hydrus

Feel my lips
As they go inside
Taking you
For a blissful ride

Quench our thirst
As you open up
Let me drink
To fill up my cup

Take your legs
Tie us in a knot
Grind my face
As you hit your spot

All of me
Is in all of you
Never stop
Theres so much to do

Play
_hydrus

Roll right over
And find your way
I have been waiting
All night and day

Let me ease
Your every care
Close your eyes
Lets disappear

In this moment
Theres only us
Feel my hands
I slowly thrust

Feeling your darkness
My soul arrives
Inside your spirit
I come alive

One
_hydrus

Come closer
Stretch your hand
Under my torso
Stands your man

Take whats yours
Pull with desire
Stroke our passion
Quench your fire

Wanting
_hydrus

I disappeared
Into her world
It was all I wanted
She became my girl

In that time
I grew inside
Began to love
Also to die

Love brought pain
And endless lies
Of lives once lived
Without goodbyes

A constant storm
Of timeless doubts
Without some reason
Without one shout

I flew away
Back to my nest
Buried my soul
With their regrets

There I stayed
Nothing to tell
No prison walls
In this sentenced hell

Convicted
_hydrus

Eyes are closed
Thats where we live
The world stands still
Our hearts forgive
A quiet peace
Where we are one
Time stands still
To a never ending sun

Wishing
_hydrus

In this ocean
Where we swim
There are no waves
Her thoughts with him

She was his seashore
An open sand
Where he once laid
Became a man

It held us close
Under the stars
A new found love
Hidden the scars

And here we are
Away from earth
Our simple place
Where love was birthed

Beach
_hydrus

In mortal hands
Blessed she stands
An angelic sight
For any man

Soft the spell
As the winds explore
A carried scent
The world adores

Behind her veil
The petals bloom
Alone in sight
They never gloom

Shy in space
She seldom leaves
Hiding her trace
From any thieves

Knowing one home
Without a field
Freedom wanes
Dreams unreal

There still she stands
Away from all
Never to grow
Only to fall

Extracted
_hydrus

I was the wolf
To her rose
Quick to kill
Then quickly froze

She showed me thorns
And bloomed in light
I denned in shadows
Covered in night

Her petals warmed
Relaxed my fears
I licked her wounds
She wiped my tears

Our endless days
A tamed escape
My new found way
Had taken shape

But envy lurked
Its malice strong
Jealous snakes
Insight your wrongs

And now the moon
Beckons my all
She left our shade
For her I call

Howl
_hydrus

Her petals made him forget that she could never be his

—hydrus

And now that is all you trust

_hydrus

Be my wings
The lifting air
A boundless flight
No atmosphere

Let your feathers
Join with mine
Under our wings
Live just to climb

We are so limitless
Our hearts rejoice
No one else matters
The skies our choice

Wings
_hydrus

Bring me your wounds
And your torn out soul
I will wrap you in love
Mend you to be whole

Escape all the bruises
That bring you much harm
I will be your refuge
Just live in my arms

There will be no anguish
Or hurt with such fear
I promise you all
My actions so clear

Together we triumph
Let suffering cease
Please hold me forever
Our worlds will be free

Found
_hydrus

Why did it die
Cold in my hands
Gave it every breath
I dont understand

We never let it grow
Never let it thrive
Only you will know
Why we let it die

We
_hydrus

Come back
Be in my arms
Its where you live
Its where Im strong
Lets begin
And start again
Be my all
My first true friend

Return
_hydrus

Little feather
Falling to earth
To fly so high
Then lose its worth

Upon the soil
Beneath the weeds
You make your home
Buried with seeds

Vines quickly wrap
Engulf your fate
Your beauty trapped
No more escape

But here you are
Fallen to earth
The skies so far
You found your worth

Destiny
_hydrus

I found romance and it knew my name
Its spell took hold I played its game
My heart was slashed I felt to blame
I was all alone with no one to claim

But I am strong and life is cruel
From these ashes my soul can rule
Find someone who cares for me
A real true love etched in destiny

Reborn
_hydrus

Little bird
Why did you come
I built my cage
You just left one

I cannot feed
But I will play
Take my finger
And perch to stay

Home
_hydrus

My infinite beauty
Dressed in black
Our endless journey
Has brought me back
A traveled soul
Ridden to roar
In my heart
Her wings will soar

Raven
_hydrus

Darkness blinds as the voices creep
Lying abandoned banished from sleep
Pain in my echoes a wounded retreat
Feel so alone a saddened repeat

Yet even in blackness once the voices cease
There will always be hope a light so discreet
It listens and loves embraces to heal
Faith in yourself can overcome this ordeal

Trust
_hydrus

How can one
Love so much
A tireless care
With every touch

Never a question
Or ever a doubt
Calm in their voice
Harmless in shout

Always protecting
While holding your hand
Quietly listening
Letting you stand

Their only objective
The one that I still miss
Was to endlessly love
Always sealed with a kiss

Moments
_hydrus

In the end
You are always there
A solid force
Without compare

My distant echo
Sweet universe
You keep me grounded
Straight on my course

I sometimes waiver
Yet you will not
Steering my darkness
At every spot

On my journey
Through many sands
You always reached me
With helping hands

Voice
_hydrus

Let me listen to you laugh
Play with all the waves
Dance in the puddles
Pretend to misbehave

Be a living angel
Friended by the flowers
Rolling in their orchards
Songbirds under showers

Rolling in the grass
Kicking all the leaves
Free as the mighty
Blowing through the trees

Never lose your passion
Always be yourself
Living is worth living
Your happiness is wealth

Believe
_hydrus

Healing does not come from

Thank You

Thank you to all of you
who continue on this journey with me.
I hope that my writings touch your soul
and at times takes you to a place of
familiarity and sometimes reflection.

Thank you also to my devoted Ravens.
All of you continuously amaze me
with your unconditional love and support.

May all of your wings grow brighter
as all of your darkness grows more beautiful.

A special thank you to Cleo @devoted_pages for her tireless devotion, creativity, relentless support and endless hard work. Thank you for everything you do and for always supporting everything _hydrus with love and care. I am so grateful for everything you do for me, for our Ravens and for all the readers.

Beauty itself
is but the sensible image of the infinite.

Francis Bacon

Also by _hydrus

ENDVISIBLE

A collection of poems about the endless feeling of being invisible while going through the emotions and sometimes cruelties of life. Illustrated by the author's own photography, this book guides us through grief, loss and love in a dark and inspiring way typical to how Hydrus's writing helps us cope with reality.

AWAKEND

Tarots cards, much like poems, have the ability to paint a vivid picture of what once was or what could be. They delve into the subtleties that we all carry within ourselves and the secrets that make us who we are.

AwakEND is an immersion into the world of tarot and its mysteries. Read it one way, then another, and let the words guide you into the meaning of each card. Allow chance and curiosity to accompany you on this incredible journey and let your heart awaken to hope even after having thought everything was lost...

And who knows what secrets you might find out about yourself...

DARK**END**

Is a small look into the world I call my reality.
Through poems, photography and art, I try to capture the ups and downs of this voyage we call life, and sometimes I refer to it as just existing.
Embedded in my words are stories of emotions and feelings that range from the darkest of moments to times of having some type of hope for resolve.

Life is raw and ever-evolving, and we always seem to put ourselves last overall. Time proves to be quite relentless. I hope that we all find common ground through our everyday struggles and in the end, understand that love, although painful at times, can provide so many answers.

So the question then becomes *"how can we better love ourselves?"*

HEART**END**

Is about how we experience love and some of the journeys we embark on when love strikes our heart. It's about the numerous complex phases and ever changing stages of the purest human emotions.
It might be a first kiss, a new romance, a guilty pleasure or a sense of loss but love always helps us reach the heavens or crash down upon its shores.
Love gives even when it takes,
it heals and embeds its mark and sculpts us into who we are.

"We all open our hearts and in the end this is the love we bleed." _*hydrus*

ENDTHOLOGY

Is a collection of poems drawn up from experiences, thoughts, and emotions. Not everything in the world is dark, but many times we live without any light. We lose ourselves in what we consider our reality. Our souls forget what is important. At the same time, we rejoice when we regain our passion and our inner light.

We might live many lives, but which one will you always remember?

What memories will we ink?

What will have true meaning?

How will we live our END?

_hydrus

About The Author

Anonymous poet, photographer and artist,
Hydrus documents through his poems the darkness and the
glimmers of life taunting us when we are in the shadows,
as well as many of the little things which make a colossal impact
on who we are.

Connect with _hydrus:

Website: www.hydruspoetry.com
Instagram: @hydruspoetry
Facebook: www.facebook.com/hydruspoetry
Redbubble Merchandise:
www.redbubble.com/people/hydruspoetry/explore

Your beautiful
darkness
is as endless
as the light
you have buried
in your heart.

_hydrus

CPSIA information can be obtained
at www.ICGtesting.com
Printed in the USA
LVHW011701260322
714494LV00006B/177